# What's the matter, Maya?

Also in the Definitely Daisy series:

# What's the matter, Maya?

Jenny Oldfield

Illustrated by
Lauren Child

*Hodder*
*Children's*
*Books*

a division of Hodder Headline Limited

For Joe, Fran and Lizzie

Text copyright © Jenny Oldfield 2001
Illustrations copyright © Lauren Child 2001

First published in Great Britain in 2001
by Hodder Children's Books

10 9 8 6 5 4 3 2 1

A Catalogue record for this book is available from
the British Library

ISBN 0 340 78503 9

Printed and bound in Great Britain

Hodder Children's Books
a division of Hodder Headline Ltd
338 Euston Road
London NW1 3BH

# One

'Aw, Mum!' Daisy Morelli pouted over her pasta.

'Daisy, don't speak with your mouth full.' Her mother jiggled baby Mia on her hip. 'And try not to make that horrible noise when you eat your spaghetti.'

*Munch-suck-munch-gulp!* 'But Mum, *why* can't I have a sleepover?'

Angie offered a spoonful of tomato sauce

to Mia. Mia tasted it, turned to Daisy and sprayed the bright red sauce all over her sister's school shirt.

'Daisy, didn't I tell you to get changed out of your uniform?' Angie sighed, trying again with the spoon and the baby.

*How come Mia spits and* I *get told off?* Daisy wondered. She rubbed at the splattered sauce with the end of her tie.

'Daisy!' Angie warned. 'Go and get changed. Put your shirt in the washing-basket.'

' 'S not fair,' Daisy grumbled, standing up from the table. 'Anyway, you still haven't told me why you won't let me have a sleepover tomorrow night.'

As Mia burbled and blew bright red bubbles, her mother began a list of the reasons why not.

'Because, one – you didn't brush your teeth this morning. Two – your room looks like a bomb dropped. Three – you lost your pencil-case, which is the third time in two weeks and I can't afford to keep on buying new ones. Four—'

'OK, OK.' Daisy broke in. 'So why don't you just send me back to where I came from and ask for a new girl!'

'Daisy!' Angie sounded shocked. Mia stared at her angry sister with her big brown eyes.

Sometimes Daisy came out with things she didn't really mean. This was one of them. 'On second thoughts; just send me back, full-stop. You've already got Mia, and she never does anything wrong!'

It was true, Daisy told herself. Once upon a time, before Mia showed up and spoiled things, she could invite her friends to sleepovers whenever she wanted, whatever she'd done wrong. Now her mum didn't let her get away with anything.

'Daisy!' Angie said again, only louder. 'Don't be silly!'

Mia's messy lips trembled. Then she opened her mouth and wailed. The sauce dribbled down her chin on to her yellow duckling bib.

'There now, you've upset your sister. Go to your room and do your homework while I sort Mia out. I'll speak to you later.'

At the dreaded words, "I'll speak to you later!", Daisy stomped to the door. Then she risked one last attempt. 'Just two friends!' she pleaded.

'Daisy!'

'*One* friend...?' (in a little, sad, lonely voice to make her mum feel guilty).

'For the last time, no sleepover!' (in a loud, I'm-at-the-end-of-my-tether voice).

So Daisy flounced out and slammed the door behind her. She went straight into the kitchen of the Pizza Palazzo to find her dad at work.

'*O, sole mio!*' Gianni sang in Italian. He threw a lump of pizza dough on to a floured board and gave it some karate chops. '*Lah-lah la-la!*'

Daisy approached him through a cloud of

white flour. 'Da-ad!' she began sweetly.

Onions fried in the pan, garlic hung in long strings from a hook on the wall. There was a smell of herbs, tomatoes and melted cheese.

Gianni looked up. 'Daisy *mia!*' he cried, swirling the pizza dough on the flat of his broad hand. 'Have you come to help in the kitchen?'

Shaking her head, she mumbled that she had horrible maths homework to do. 'But Da-ad!' she wheedled, flashing her big brown eyes just like Mia did. 'Please, please, please can you persuade Mum to let me have a sleepover?'

'A sleeping-over, eh?' her dad said pleasantly. He punched and chopped at the soft dough, humming as he worked. 'You want friends to come visit, eat pizza, play games?'

'Yeah, tomorrow!' she said eagerly. She could rely on her dad to smile and say yes.

But her mum must have wired the whole house with secret microphones.

'*Daisy!*' Angie called through the closed door.

Daisy's heart sank. Foiled again.

'Don't try worming your way into your dad's good books,' came the sharp order. 'I want you to go upstairs and do your maths homework right now, if not sooner!'

'Hi, Leonie! Hi, Maya! Hi, Jade!' A cheerful voice called out above the noise of the playground first thing next morning.

Daisy kicked the football to Jimmy Black, then turned to look suspiciously at Winona Jones. Why was Winona sounding so bright and breezy, she wondered.

Jimmy dribbled past Jared and Kyle. 'Back to you, Daisy!' he yelled. '…Daisy, where were you?'

She sprinted over the tarmac towards the goalposts painted on the stone wall. But she was way too late to take the pass.

Jimmy huffed and puffed. 'I said, where were you?'

'Sorry!' she gasped. She scooped the ball out of a nearby drain, where it had trickled once it had gone out of play.

'It was our chance to go ahead!' Jimmy rubbed it in. When it came to playing soccer, his one aim was to win. Now Daisy had blown it, just as the bell rang for the start of school.

'So-rry!' Daisy chucked him the ball. 'You'd better leave me out of your precious team next time if I'm so useless!'

Sulking, she ran towards the main building, coming up between Maya and Leonie as they strolled in with Jade and Winona.

'So that's settled, then?' Winona said. 'Seven o'clock tomorrow night?'

Jade and Maya nodded. Leonie threw an uneasy look at Daisy, which Winona saw and worked out.

'Oh, yeah; sorry, Daisy. I'm only allowed to invite three people.' Tossing her fair curls behind her shoulders, Winona waltzed ahead.

'Invite three people to what?' Daisy whispered to Leonie with a sinking feeling. (Mizz Bright-and-Breezy. Hi, everyone! ...Oh, sorry, Daisy, I can't include you!)

'Winona asked us to a sleepover at her place tomorrow night,' Leonie confessed.

The answer stopped Daisy in her tracks. She let crowds of kids overtake her, including Jimmy and the rest of the soccer team. 'And you said yes?' she asked Leonie.

'Well – yeah.' Leonie shuffled her feet and looked at the ground. 'You already told us that your mum wouldn't let you have anyone to stay this weekend.'

'But Winona-Stupid-Jones didn't know that!'

Two teachers went by, their arms piled with books. Leonie seized the chance to escape from Daisy by running to hold open the door for them.

'Thank you, Leonie dear,' Mrs Hunt said.

Daisy waited until they'd gone in. Then she grabbed Leonie's arm. 'When you said yes to

Winona, did you already know that she wasn't planning to invite me?'

'Erm – no, not exactly,' Leonie squirmed. Then she pulled free. 'Listen, Daisy. Don't make it such a big deal. It's only a little sleepover.'

'Yeah, and Winona did it on purpose to annoy me.' A black cloud came and settled over Daisy's head. Life was lousy when your mum got mega-strict and your friends left you out. Not to mention the look on Jimmy's face when she'd missed that easy pass.

'Come along, Daisy!' As Leonie slipped off inside the building, Miss Ambler came puffing up behind. She carried two heavy bags and a bundle of rounders bats. 'Open the door for me, there's a good girl.'

Taken by surprise, Daisy fell up the last two steps and toppled against the swing-door. She landed face-down on the prickly mat. Yeah, life was definitely lousy.

'Pick yourself up,' Rambler-Ambler told her crossly. No asking if she was OK. Instead, the teacher stepped right over Daisy into the entrance hall. 'And hurry along while I call at the office to pick up the register. If it was anyone else in the class, I'd ask them to do it for me. But I'm afraid, Daisy Morelli, that you just can't be trusted!'

*Witchy-witchy magic! Make me a puppet!* Daisy decided to cheer herself up during Art.

She grabbed a lump of pink modelling-clay and made it into the rough shape of a human figure. A head on a fat sausage

body, plus two
plump arms and
legs. Then she stuck
worms of yellow
clay on top of the
head to make long
hair. It didn't look
much like Winona
Jones, but Daisy
didn't care. Witches

didn't bother about stuff like making things
seem real.

'Hubble-bubble, witchy-woo!

Eyes of toads and lizards too!'

Daisy didn't know what it meant, but it
sounded good. Now she was ready to cast a
spell.

'Make Winona's golden curls fall out one by
one!' she cursed, tugging at the doll's locks.

She looked up hopefully at Winona, who
was busy on the far side of the room making
flowers out of pink tissue paper and glue.

Nope, her hair was still hanging in neat,
shiny ringlets.

'Hubble-bubble, witchy-woo,

Make Winona stick her hands with glue!' Daisy chanted.

Across the room, the Sleepover Queen cut and pasted perfect flowers.

*Huh!* Daisy grew desperate. She seized a pencil and began to jab the sharp end into the little doll's feet.

'Hubble-bubble, witchy woes,

Make pins and needles in her toes!'

'Ouch!' Winona cried suddenly. She glared at Kyle Peterson, who had just passed by. 'Miss Ambler, Kyle just trod on my foot!'

Hmm, maybe there was something in this witchy magic after all! Daisy grinned to herself.

She was so busy hubble-bubbling that she didn't notice the teacher patrolling nearby.

'Daisy Morelli, what on earth do you call this!' Miss Ambler cried, suddenly pouncing on the tiny model of Winona.

Daisy swallowed hard. Somehow, 'Please,
Miss, it's a sculpture of Winona-Stupid-
Jones!' didn't sound like the smart thing to
say.

'Don't tell us; let's guess!' Ambler held up
the model for the rest of the class to see.
'Perhaps it's a piece of modern abstract art
called "Pink and Yellow – er – Splodge"?'

A few people like Kyle, Nathan and
Winona laughed at the feeble joke.

*Hah-hah!* Daisy frowned. With her new-
found itchy-witchy powers, she knew they'd
all soon be laughing on the other side of
their faces.

'Look at the sleeves of your shirt!' Miss
Ambler pointed out the gungey pink blobs of
modelling clay stuck to Daisy's cuffs. 'And see
here, you've even managed to get the horrid
stuff on poor Herbie!'

Once more, Daisy was too slow to stop the
teacher. She watched in horror as Rambler
slammed Winona down then seized Daisy's

favourite stuffed hamster by one ear.

Herbie suffered in silence. He just stared down at Daisy with his one good eye and a look that seemed to say, *"Get me out of this mess!"*

Dangling an unhappy Herbie in front of them, Miss Boring Snoring wagged a finger. 'He's covered in the stuff!' she exclaimed examining, the sagging beanie babe pet more closely before she whisked him away to her front desk, Miss Ambler remembered one of her rules. 'That's why we have a routine of clearing the tops of our desks before every art lesson,' she reminded them primly. 'If we leave anything lying around, this is what happens!'

*"Save me!"* Herbie cried in a faint voice. At least, it seemed to Daisy that this was what he *would* have said if squidgy stuffed hamsters could talk. *"She's pulling my ear off and making me feel sick! And it's all your fault!"*

'Please Miss, I'll remember next time!'

Daisy made a feeble effort to come to Herbie's aid.

But Ambler wasn't in the mood to give her a second chance.

'There won't *be* a next time,' she said severely, pulling open her desk drawer and dropping Herbie roughly inside. *Plomp!* He landed with a thud. 'I'm confiscating your hamster for the rest of this term!'

Ambler was in a mood, thanks to Daisy. The rest of the class ducked their heads and got on quietly with their work.

'B-b-but!' Daisy stammered.

Without Herbie to talk to last thing at night she was lost. Now who would she confide in about the deep, deep pain of being left out of Winona's sleepover? And who would listen to her moans about baby Mia being her mum and dad's favourite if Herbie wasn't squatting on her pillow, blinking sleepily at her with his one wise eye?

'Daisy Morelli, don't "but" me!' Miss Ambler insisted, slamming the drawer shut.

'You know the rule perfectly well. My decision is final. Herbie stays here with me until Christmas!'

# Two

'What's the matter, Daisy?' Maya asked.

She'd come up quietly while Daisy watched the school soccer team score the first goal against Hilltop Juniors in the Schools Saturday League.

All along the touchline, supporters of Jimmy's team jumped up and down and cheered. Jimmy the goalscorer did a lap of honour round the pitch.

'Nothing's the matter,' Daisy replied huffily. She had her evil eye fixed on Winona Jones who was flouncing around in a frilly white blouse by the goalposts with her poncey poodle, Lulu.

('Daisy *mia*, don't sulk,' her dad had advised when she'd told him her problems the night before. 'Winona's a nice girl. Let her invite friends to her house for a sleeping-over. Try not to be jealous. It spoils your smiley face.')

'Are you sulking about Winona's sleepover?' Maya asked now.

'Nope.' Daisy tossed her tangled mop of hair back from her face.

Maya stayed quiet while the teams took the ball back to the centre line and began again. 'I'm sorry she left you out,' she murmured as Jared went in for a tackle.

'Jimmy-Jimmy-Jimmy!' Winona led the cheers for Woodbridge Junior's heroic captain. 'Jim-Jim-Jim!'

'I don't care,' Daisy told Maya. 'I didn't

want to go anyway!'

Maya hovered. 'I still wish you were coming,' she insisted, fiddling with the end of her long black plait. 'Maybe I could ask Winona to invite you after all…'

'No way!' Daisy's loud yelp made Lulu turn and bark. 'Like, DON'T DO THAT, OK?'

Startled, Maya stared at Daisy with her gentle brown eyes. She gave a hurried nod, then backed away.

('This is what happens when you sulk,' Daisy's dad had told her when he came in to say goodnight. 'You make your friends unhappy. They leave you all alone.'

He'd been worse than Herbie at handing out the unwelcome advice. Daisy had tossed and turned in bed for hours. She'd woken up in a worse mood than ever.)

'One-nil, one-nil!' Winona crowed as she raised her arms and swayed from side to side.

Daisy saw that her arch-enemy was too busy leading the chants to notice that the caretaker's bulldog had put in an appearance. Lennox was padding heavily across the grass towards Lulu, huffing and puffing as he advanced. His fat face wobbled, his legs bowed out under the weight of his barrel-shaped body.

*Huf-huff-hgugh-hgugh* – Lennox made a bee-line for the poodle.

*...'OK, pal, this is my turf!' The unshaven gangster snarled at the lightweight newcomer. His muscles bulged through his white T-shirt, his eyes mean and bloodshot.*

*The well-dressed stranger in the light raincoat blanked Fat Lennox. He drained his glass and pushed it across the bar for a second drink.*

*Other customers picked up their hats and drifted away. They were tough, but not that tough. When Lennox was in a mean mood, no way did they want to stick around.*

'Maybe you didn't hear me,' he growled. An ugly sneer parted his lips to reveal rows of sharp teeth. 'I said, this is my patch. I don't want no punks buttin' in!'

This time the stranger turned slowly towards the gangster, coolly checking him for weapons. 'Since when was it a crime for a guy to order a couple of drinks at a bar?' he asked.

Bam! Lennox let rip with a punch that would have felled a buffalo.

The bartender grabbed the whiskey bottle from the bar and bobbed out of sight.

The cool stranger ducked.

Whizz! The punch missed its target. Lennox staggered and fell against a stool. The stranger caught him with an uppercut to the jaw which sent him sprawling...

Grrrrufff! The overweight bulldog bared his teeth and charged across the grass at Lulu.

The poodle yapped back, then ran to hide behind Winona.

Realising what was going on, Winona stopped chanting for her team and turned to stand squarely between Lennox and her precious Lulu.

'Go away, Lennox!' she said crossly. 'Leave Lulu alone!'

Faced with fierce Winona, Fat Lennox's growl died in his throat. It turned to a choking, wheezy sound – *Huh-huh-huff.*

*Hmm.* Even Daisy was impressed. It took nerve to face up to the caretaker's slavering dog.

From behind her owner's back, Lulu gave a smug yap.

'Get that dog off my soccer pitch!' a voice roared.

Daisy turned from the soccer action to see Bernie King lumbering towards Winona. The caretaker spent all his spare time grooming and clipping the grass, marking out the pitch and repairing the nets. He went mad if you so much as set foot on it without permission. And now he'd spotted Lulu prancing about on at least three stalks of grass.

Daisy grinned to herself. *Get out of* that *one, Win-oh-na!*

Mizz Perfect went pale when she saw Bernie's burly figure. His big boots clomped towards her. He shook his fist and yelled.

'Offside!' the Hilltop supporters protested as Jimmy put a second ball in the back of their net.

The referee ignored them. 'Goal!' he insisted.

'Two-nil, two-nil!' Woodbridge fans cheered, this time without Winona.

'That dog is on my pitch!' King cried. 'Put it on a lead or I'll report you to the Head!'

Winona scooped her permed and pampered poodle into her arms. She pointed at the wheezy bulldog. 'Lennox is on the pitch too!'

Fat Lennox had sat on the grass with his rear end and stumpy tail just inside the white line. He struggled to catch his breath after the failed attack on Lulu.

Bernie came right up to her and glared. 'Lennox has permission,' he insisted. 'That dog knows how to behave. I've trained him myself. All right?'

Winona knew there was no arguing with this. Bernie was King of Woodbridge Junior. Whatever he said went.

'Right then, Lulu and I are going!' she retorted, her pooch tucked under one arm.

'We know when we're not wanted!'

As Lennox panted and Bernie glared, Winona set off quick march towards the gate. But seeing Daisy standing alone on the touchline, she swerved towards her.

'Hi, Daisy!' she chirped.

'Hrrrgh,' Daisy growled.

The poodle pricked her ears and looked out for Lennox.

'Trust Bernie Stupid King!' Winona sighed.

'Hurrgg.' Daisy made it clear that she wasn't in the mood to talk. She narrowed her eyes and thought bad thoughts.

*Eyes of newt, ears of frog,*
*Make Winona lose her dog!*

But Winona changed the subject. 'Listen, I've been thinking,' she began, still hugging Lulu tight. 'And I decided that not inviting you to my sleepover wasn't a very nice thing to do.'

Daisy shrugged and sniffed.

'So I asked Mum if I could have an extra person and she said yes. That means you can come!'

'Has Maya said anything?' Daisy asked quickly.

'No. Why?' Winona blushed. 'Even if she has, what difference does it make? Do you want to come to my house, or not?'

Daisy tossed her head. 'Sorry, I can't make it. I'm busy.' *Yeah; busy doing the washing up. Busy making my bed and tidying my room!*

'Oh!' Winona's face fell. 'What are you doing?'

'Things!' Daisy looked away towards the pitch. Hilltop had just scored and were traipsing back to the centre line.

'What things?'

'We're having a big party at my house,' Daisy lied. 'My Italian grandma is coming, plus my three uncles and two aunts with all their kids. That's sixteen cousins. There'll be food and wine and music, and we'll probably stay up all night. Like I said, it's a mega party!'

'Yeah.' Winona nodded and sighed. She turned away, ready to move off. 'Well, sorry you can't come…'

Daisy knew she'd overdone it. She darted after Winona and Lulu. 'Hang on a second. Which night are we talking about?'

'Tonight,' Winona reminded her. 'Why? When's your party?'

'*Tomorrow* night!' Daisy claimed, as if she'd suddenly realised that they'd got their wires crossed. 'My grandma flies in from Rome at midday, with all the aunts and uncles!'

'Then you can come to my sleepover after all?' Winona seemed truly pleased. 'That's great. Come to my house at seven. Bring a sleeping bag and some snacks for a midnight feast!'

*Do you think Winona knew you were lying?* Herbie winked at Daisy with his one eye as she packed her bag with pyjamas and packets of crisps.

She'd run through it word for word for him, as soon as she'd snuck into school after the soccer match and snatched him from Miss Ambler's drawer.

... "Mystery of the Missing Hamster!" The story was splashed across the front pages of the Sunday newspapers. "Hamster Heist Leaves Police Guessing!" "Herbie Escapes from Top Security Prison. Police Suspect Outside Help!"

Daisy Fingers Morelli smiled as she read the reports. The dumb cops would never work out how she'd done it. They needed brains, and that was the one thing they were short of.

Herbie One Eye sat in the easy chair across the room, legs crossed and with his arms behind his head, taking it easy.

'Listen to this!' Fingers read the report out loud. '"News of the escape broke late last night, when Herbie One Eye's jailer, Officer Louise Ambler, turned up to begin *a new shift. Straight away she realised something was wrong. The door to the hamster's cell was ajar and she soon discovered that the prisoner was missing.*

*' "Despite setting off the alarm, no trace of the escaped convict has so far been found. Police Superintendant Waymann of Woodgate Police Department has warned the public not to approach the hamster or his accomplice, both of whom may be armed and dangerous…" '*

'I don't care if Winona believed me or not!' Daisy insisted, smiling as she stuffed a bag of jelly beans into her jeans pocket. 'Making up that stuff about the party made it look like I was too busy to bother with Winona's diddly little sleepover. It's like I'm doing her a favour by agreeing to go.

*But you've never met your Italian grandmother!* Herbie's stare brought Daisy up short. *The last time she visited was*

*before you were born, remember!'*

'Sshh!' Daisy hissed. Then she threatened her goody-goody hamster. 'If you don't keep quiet, I'll… I'll… I won't take you to the sleepover. I'll leave you here all alone in a big cold bed!'

But she took Herbie after all. What was the point of springing him from jail if she had to leave him behind? So into the bag he went, squidged between her pyjama top and a packet of smoky bacon flavour corn snacks.

'Better not let Mum see you covered in

sticky pink bits,' she told him. The more she picked at the modelling clay to tidy him up, the balder he grew. 'She'd chuck you in the washing machine and you'd have to stay behind while I went out.'

*Don't worry, I'm used to being smuggled out.* With a quick wink, Herbie settled himself down for the journey.

'Daisy, are you ready yet?' Angie called upstairs.

'Coming!' she replied.

'Did you brush your hair?'

'Yep!' – Two quick whisks with the hairbrush.

'And clean your teeth?'

'Yep!' – Using her forefinger, Daisy rubbed her front teeth until they squeaked.

'Have you been to the loo and packed a clean pair of…?'

'Ye-es!' Daisy appeared at the top of the stairs. She took them two at a time then jumped the last four. 'Ready!'

'About time too,' her mum sighed. She carried Mia into the kitchen and told Gianni that she'd had no time to dress the baby for going out, so he would have to look after her while she took Daisy to her sleepover.

Mia bawled as Angie slipped her into her high-chair. She raised her fat arms and pleaded not to be left.

'Coo-coo!' Gianni tickled her chin with his floury hands.

'Waaaaagghh!' Mia wailed.

*Ping!* The bell on the restaurant door sounded as new customers came in and ordered four pizzas.

'*Mama mia!*' Daisy's dad cried. 'How many pairs of hands do they think I have?'

'Hushh!' Angie soothed Mia. 'Mummy won't be long.'

'Woaaaagghhh!' the baby roared.

' "*O, sole mio!*" ' Gianni began to sing to drown out the noise. He chopped and fried, stirred and baked.

'Mu-um!' Daisy tugged at Angie's arm. She needed to escape from this madhouse and get to the sleepover.

Her dad sang and made pizzas. Her mum flapped. Mia boo-hooed.

'Come on, Mum,' Daisy insisted. 'Let's go!'

# Three

Winona's house was next to Maya's on Woodbridge Road. From the back bedroom window in the daylight you could see a neat, narrow garden, then the open green space of the school playing field and the grey stone buildings beyond.

But now it was dark, and the only light that shone through the pitch-black gloom came from the caretaker's small cottage beside the school.

'I wouldn't like to live here,' Daisy confessed to Leonie after they'd spent ten minutes spying with Mr Jones's binoculars on Bernie King. 'When I go home I like to forget about school.'

'Me too.' Leonie lived next to the park. She and her sister could play there whenever they felt like it.

'I'm still hungry. Someone pass me the Zooms!' Daisy called across the dark room.

They were having the secret midnight food fest that Winona had promised – crisps and chocolate, corn snacks and pink marshmallows. Winona's mum and dad had gone to bed an hour before, not knowing what the girls had planned.

'Sssshhhh!' Winona hissed. She flicked on her torch to search for the packet of corn snacks, found it in one of Jade's trainers and chucked it towards the windowsill.

Daisy dived to catch it, missed and toppled off the windowsill. She landed with a bump on Maya's sleeping-bag.

'Ouch!' The sleeping-bag was already occupied.

'Sorry, Maya!' Daisy picked herself up then scrambled on the floor for the snack. 'Shine the torch over here!' she told Winona.

The yellow beam shone up the wall, across the ceiling, then dipped down to the hump that was Maya.

'Not there – here!' Daisy ordered. 'Never mind, I've found it!' Clutching the crushed packet, she clambered back on to the wide window ledge beside Leonie.

'Hey, mind the last little bit of chocolate!' Leonie warned.

Too late. Daisy sat right on it. 'Huh. I was saving that for pudding!' She began to giggle as she and Leonie tried to scrape the squashed chocolate off her pyjamas.

'Will you two please be quiet!' Winona whispered.

Still giggling, Daisy glanced up to see Winona in a white nightdress, standing with her ear pressed against the wall.

'Ooh, it's a ghost!' Leonie pretended to be scared.

Daisy laughed. 'A gho-o-ost!' she wailed and clutched Leonie's hand. '*Woooooo!*'

' 'S'not funny!' Winona said crossly. 'I thought I heard a noise from Mum and Dad's room!'

'Now I'm really scared!' Daisy giggled. Mrs Jones was a grown-up version of Winona; the same wavy blonde hair, the long eyelashes, the neat-and-petite look. And she was super-strict.

'*Pppphhhuh!*' Leonie couldn't stop another laugh from popping out. She jumped down from the windowsill, clean over Maya, into the middle of Winona's white, furry rug.

'Hey, watch out for my marshmallows!' Jade cried.

'Urgh!' Leonie had landed smack on them. She felt them squidge between her toes.

'Oh no!' Winona wailed. She swung her torch towards Jade. 'Don't tell me you left them on the rug!'

'Sorry, Winona!' Jade shrank away from the beam of light .

'My mum will kill me!' Shoving Leonie out of the way and dropping to her knees, Winona began to scrub furiously at the pink sticky patch. 'This is the last time I invite anyone except Maya to my house for a sleepover!'

'Hey, what did I do wrong?' Jade protested.

'What was that noise?' By this time Daisy had definitely heard movement from next door.

'Ha-ha-ha!' Leonie thought she was still joking. She hopped around the room, holding her foot to her mouth and trying to lick marshmallow from between her toes.

Daisy listened again. 'No, honestly – I can hear something!'

'Me too,' Maya and Jade agreed.

For a split second they all froze.

*Click!* The handle turned on Mr and Mrs Jones's bedroom door.

*Whoosh!* Leonie, Jade, Daisy and Winona shot into their sleeping-bags. They pulled them over their heads and pretended to be asleep.

*Click!* Winona's door opened and Mrs Jones looked in.

*Zzzz-zzzz!*

Leonie produced a realistic snore.

Winona's mum listened, gave a puzzled "hmmm", then left without closing the door.

Slowy five heads peered out from their sleeping-bags and stared at the chink of light from the landing.

'Close!' Daisy sighed.

'Too close!' Winona hissed. 'Honestly, I'm going to be in dead trouble when Mum sees the rug!'

'OK, Daisy and I will be good from now on,' Leonie promised. 'The only place we'll put food will be in our mouths!'

Suddenly the idea of uneaten Zooms on the windowsill made Daisy's mouth water. Realising that she still hadn't had enough to eat, yet afraid to get out of bed, she fished under her pillow for the bag of jelly beans she'd hidden there when she unpacked. But instead of sweets, she found good old Herbie.

'Hey, Herb. I hope you didn't eat all my blackcurrant flavours!' she whispered. Perching him on the outside of her sleeping-bag, she fished again. Soon she was popping the sugary beans into her mouth and experimenting in the dark to see if she could guess the taste.

Strawberry ice-cream… white chocolate… lime and lemon. In the warm darkness of the crowded room, Daisy tempted the hamster with each sweet before she gulped it down.

*Zzz-zzz!* This time the snoring was real. It

came from Winona's corner – long, loud and definitely pig-like.

*Hah!* Daisy thought. Here was something to tease Mizz Perfect about next time she was being a pain. Blackcurrent (*yum!*)… raspberry sundae… pistachio…

*Snuffle-snuffle-snuffle.* All of a sudden Daisy felt hot breath on her cheek. She turned over to find that Lulu had sneaked through the open door and crept right up to her.

'Gerroff!' Daisy mumbled with a mouthful of jelly beans.

But the poodle had smelt the sweets. She put out her little pink tounge and sat up on her hind legs to beg.

*Ah, cute!* Softening, Daisy dipped into her jelly bean bag and offered Lulu a peach melba flavour.

*Ooolch!* The bean disappeared in a milli-second. Lulu licked her lips and begged for more.

'Just one!' Trying to sound stern this time,

Daisy offered the poodle a liquorice flavour.

*Olch!* Even faster than before, Lulu gulped it down.

'No more,' Daisy insisted, trying to shoo the dog off her sleeping-bag. 'Go away, Lulu. I said no more!'

The pesky pooch pushed and snuffled, wriggling her head inside Daisy's sleeping bag to get to them.

From his position on the pillow, Herbie's cross look warned that this latest little incident would end in tears.

'Ouch!' Daisy winced as Lulu dug her pointed teeth into the tip of her finger. Wrestling her hand free, she tipped Herbie off the pillow and sent Lulu tottering back towards Maya.

Herbie tumbled on to the polished floor, rolled and slid up to the surprised poodle, who regained her balance in time to spot the furry object skate into her. Quick as a flash she seized Herbie by the ear and bounded from the room.

…'These creatures attack in the dead of night,' Professor Morelli told the group of worried explorers. 'They choose their victims carefully, picking out the weakest member of the herd.'

'But Professor, why have we never come across the White Haired Woolly Poodlion before?' her anxious guide asked.

The group had gathered around the campfire in a small clearing in the jungle. They were dressed in white shorts and safari hats. Most were badly shaken by what they had just seen.

Only Professor Morelli kept a clear head. 'Because they live in the very deepest part of the rainforest,' she explained. 'It is a region unknown to man. In fact, we are only just beginning to understand the habits of these rare and extremely dangerous giant beasts.'

'And you're the world expert,' another

explorer pointed out. 'So tell us, Professor, will the Poodlion kill and eat its prey immediately? In other words, how long do we have to save the life of the poor Hamsterus Beani-Babius?'

Professor Morelli frowned. 'We have five minutes precisely before the Poodlion reaches its lair. Then and only then will it sink its fangs into the helpless victim. We must act quickly and face the fact that any attempt at rescue will put us in danger of our own lives!'

'You mean, the Poodlion will attack and kill humans?' a third expedition member asked in a shaky voice.

Morelli nodded grimly. 'It's fearless. So if anyone here wants to stay behind, I would completely understand.'

'We're with you, Professor!' The whole group gathered their courage and prepared to hack their way through the jungle.

'Then follow me!' she cried.

Daisy leaped from her sleeping-bag and shot on to the landing. Lulu had already reached the bottom of the stairs. Daisy caught a glimpse of Herbie hanging limply from the poodle's mouth as she screeched around the corner into the kitchen.

So Daisy took the stairs two at a time. *Thud-thud-thud.*

The poodle charged on with the hamster. With one giant bound she jumped on to the draining-board and pawed at the window. It opened wide enough for her to squeeze through. Then she leaped into the garden and vanished once more.

Daisy didn't hestitate. Vaulting on to the sink, she slithered head-first through the narrow gap, wriggling her shoulders and feeling with her hands for something solid to land on.

*Splosh! Trust Winona's family to have a*

*fish-pond by their kitchen window!*

Daisy found herself covered in slimy pond-weed and soaked to the skin. A big orange fish swam up and began to nibble her toe. Of course, Lulu knew about the watery landing and had jumped clear. She'd dashed on with Herbie to the end of the garden and been swallowed by the darkness.

Picking herself up, Daisy climbed out of the pond and followed. And now she could hear a mysterious scratching, scrabbling noise, as if sharp paws were scratching at the loose earth. Yes, that was it – Daisy barged into a garden bench and somersaulted over it – Lulu was digging!

Daisy's heart thumped. The dog planned to bury the hamster!

Frantically she searched the dark garden for a white blob. *Please let me find Herbie before it's too late!* Blundering on, she tumbled into a prickly bush, fought her way through, then came across the sight she'd been dreading.

Lulu's hole was already deep. She'd piled up loose earth behind her and was getting ready to dump Herbie in it.

'Oh no you don't!' Daisy cried, launching herself at the poodle. She jumped so suddenly that Lulu dropped the hamster in surprise. Daisy scooped him up and clutched him to her. Herbie was safe!

'Daisy Morelli, what *are* you doing?' Mrs Jones looked down on the wet, grubby, scratched mess that was Daisy. Her floaty white dressing gown stood out in the dark garden and her long fair hair fell in curls over her shoulders. The look on her face said that she could hardly believe what she saw.

'Lulu kidnapped Herbie!' Daisy gasped. She noticed that there was by now no sign of the cunning pooch, who must have made her getaway under the fence into the school playing field.

'But what are *you* doing?' Mrs Jones said again.

'Rescuing him!' That disgusted look made

Daisy feel two inches high. Now she knew where Winona got it from.

There was a long, silent stare. Winona's mum took in Daisy's muddy pyjamas and the sad sight of a mangled Herbie. 'Well, I suggest you get back to bed,' Mrs jones said at last. 'We'll have to sort this out in the morning.'

Sunday morning came. Mrs Jones rang Angie Morelli to apologise for the state of Daisy's pyjamas. I'm afraid Daisy was involved in an after-dark adventure,' she explained. 'No doubt she'll tell you all about it when she gets back home!'

Daisy frowned at her cereal bowl. Now she was in BIG trouble.

'Never mind – you rescued Herbie,' Maya reminded her as the front doorbell rang.

When Mrs Jones answered it, she found Bernie King standing on her doorstep holding a dirty bone in his broad hand.

'I take it this belongs to you!' he bellowed.

'Er – there must be some mistake…'

Winona's mum dithered.

'No. This is definitely your bone.' The caretaker made her take it. 'to be more precise your *dog's* bone.'

'B-but…'

'You own a white poodle, don't you?'

Daisy, Winona, Jade, Maya and Leonie crowded around the door to listen. They saw that Bernie's face looked like thunder and that his hands were shaking with rage.

'Y-yes…' Mrs Jones stammered. 'What has Lulu done?'

'Only gone and dug a hole and buried her bone in my soccer pitch!' Bernie exploded. 'She's ruined weeks of hard work, that's all!

# Four

'There's not just one hole, there's three!'
Jimmy said in dismay.

It was first thing Monday morning, and the
mystery of the ruined soccer pitch had
deepened.

'What's gonna happen to Saturday's
knock-out cup competition?' Daisy wondered.
'The teams can't play if there's massive great
holes all over the place!'

Jimmy shrugged and frowned at the three rough pyramids of black earth scattered across the smooth grass. 'No wonder Bernie blew his top,' he muttered.

'Yeah, and that was when there was only one.' Daisy had described to Jimmy how the caretaker had fumed like a volcano on the Jones's doorstep.

'My dog doesn't eat bones!' Winona's mum had told him primly. 'And she's never buried anything in her entire life!'

'Erm—' Daisy had been about to remind her of the after-dark adventure with Herbie but Leonie had given her a sharp jab with her elbow. 'Don't even think about it!' she'd hissed. 'Not unless you want to be in Scary Megan Jones's bad books for ever and ever!'

So Daisy had reluctantly decided to keep her mouth shut.

'All dogs eat bones,' Bernie had insisted. 'And I saw it with my own eyes – your poncey white poodle legging it across my pitch in the middle of the night. First thing this morning, I look out of my window and what do I see? One dirty great hole. One bone!' Steam seemed to come out of his ears as he repeated the charge.

To the girls' surprise, Mrs Jones had managed to stand up to him. 'Let me get this clear,' she'd said, cool as a cucumber. 'You glance out of your window in the dead of night. You think you see a pale-coloured animal running across the field. But from that distance in the pitch dark I don't see how you can possibly prove it was Lulu. It may even have been a cat for all we know.'

'Do cats dig holes?' Bernie had challenged.

'Certainly they do,' Mrs Jones had insisted, ready to go into detail about cats' hygiene habits.

'Yes, but do they bury *bones*?' The caretaker had said, jabbing his blunt finger at the filthy object.

By this time, Daisy had suspected he was going to go up in smoke if Mrs Jones didn't stop arguing. All that would be left of him would be a messy black patch on the doorstep. In contrast, Winona's mum had grown frostier.

She'd held up the bone between her thumb and forefinger. 'Are you suggesting that I gave this object to my poodle to eat?'

Bernie's double chin had wobbled and his face had broken out in a furious sweat.

'Strange!' Mrs Jones hadn't given him time to speak. 'Mr King, did you know that we don't have meat in this house? Douglas, Winona and I are strict vegetarians. So the bone couldn't possibly have come from here!'

'Maybe it was a mole,' Jimmy said now. 'Moles pop out of the ground and make piles of dirt, don't they?'

'True.' Daisy studied the damage. 'But moles make neater heaps. These are quite messy.' As a matter of fact, they did look exactly like the hole Lulu had dug in her own back garden to bury Herbie in. For once, she found herself edging towards Bernie King's side of an argument.

'Anyhow, I don't suppose it really matters who made them. What's important is that they don't dig any more before the big match.' Jimmy sighed, then wandered off towards the school until he spotted Maya's older brother, Kamran cutting across the field to join him.

Kamran was the goalkeeper in Woodbridge Junior's soccer team; a tall, sporty kid with glossy dark hair and a wide, white smile. 'Hey, Jimmy, did you see the ho—'

'Yeah,' he said. 'I saw 'em. Bernie went mad. He thinks it was Winona's dog.'

'You're kidding me!' Kamran stared at the holes. 'That weedy little poodle thing?'

As the boys walked off deep in discussion of the problem, Daisy turned to greet Maya, who had just come through her garden gate into the playing-field.

'Hey, Daisy, how did you get on yesterday

when you got back home?'

Daisy gave her a thumbs-down. 'Don't ask. Let's just say I nearly ended up in the washing machine with my pyjamas and Herbie.' Her mum had given her a hard time over something that simply hadn't been her fault. Daisy's 'Don't blame me, blame Lulu' line hadn't gone down well. Angie had come across with the old 'Daisy, you're a disgrace' message, then coo-cooed over messy Mia as usual.

'Tough.' Maya sounded truly sorry. 'Living next door to Lulu, I know she can be a pain at times.'

Daisy nodded hard. 'Yeah, and I bet she really *did* scoot under the fence and dig that hole, whatever Winona's mum says.'

'Oh no, I don't think so!' Maya said. Then she quickly clammed up.

'How come?' Daisy squinted curiously at her. 'Do you know something I don't?'

Maya shook her head and glanced nervously across the soccer pitch.

Turning to find out what was so interesting, Daisy spotted Bernie King marching out of his office with a spade and a bucket. Fat Lennox waddled at his heels, grumpy as ever.

'Let's go!' Maya whispered. 'C'mon, Daisy, the bell's about to go.'

'What's Bernie up to now?' Daisy waited a few moments until the gloomy caretaker reached the first untidy hole. He put down his bucket and began to shift the loose soil with his spade. As soon as the hole was full, he patted it flat, took a sod of turf from his

bucket and stamped it into the bare patch of ground.

'First-aid for the pitch!' Daisy grinned. Maybe the boys didn't need to worry about Saturday's competition after all. At this rate, the holes would be nicely patched up.

Then she realised she'd been talking to thin air because Maya had scuttled off without her. Something was bothering her. But what? Daisy took a wild guess that it had something to do with Bernie King.

'Hey, wait for me!' Daisy cried. She had to run to catch up as Maya skirted around the edge of Bernie's precious pitch without turning round. 'I said, wait for me! Maya, what on earth's wrong with you?'

'What's the matter, Maya?' Miss Ambler asked during the first lesson.

All through registration and assembly. Maya had worn a troubled look. At times, during Mrs Waymann's daily pep talk, Daisy had thought that her quiet friend had been almost about to burst into tears.

"Quiet" was the word the teachers used when they talked about Maya. Sometimes they added "Nice and" beforehand. 'Maya is so nice and quiet,' Rambler Ambler would tell Mr and Mrs Khan at parents' evenings. 'She always listens well and does her work without chattering. In fact, she's a model pupil.'

Often Ambler would finish telling Daisy off over some innocent mistake or tiny little crime like turning down the corner of a page, then say that she wished Daisy could be more like Maya. 'Maya's the sort who's bound to get on in life,' she would advise, while the model pupil blushed and buried her head in a book. 'She's a hard worker who always does as she's told; never any trouble – unlike *some* people I could mention!' Then the eyebrow would go up and the teacher would give Daisy the STARE.

*Scary stuff!* Having Maya's name rammed down her throat ought to have

turned Daisy against the goody-goody
example, but didn't. 'Unlike some people I
could mention!' In the playground Daisy
would echo Miss Boring-Snoring and arch
her eyebrow. Maya would giggle as she
went on to copy Winona's prancing walk.
'Some people are so perfect they make you
sick. But not you, Maya.' In fact, Daisy liked
her a lot. Reasons why:

   1. You could trust Maya never to dob you
in. Mega important.

   2. She was mostly serious, but that didn't
mean she couldn't take a joke.

   3. She was clever, but not mega clever.
Meaning, she could "help" you with your
homework without making you feel dumb.

   4. She was kind. Mega kind.

   Daisy finished her list. "Kind" – yeah, Maya
was definitely that.

   So when Miss Ambler went up to her desk
during creative writing and asked her what
was the matter, Daisy paid special attention.

   'Nothing, Miss,' Maya murmured.

'You're very quiet this morning,' the teacher commented. 'And I can tell that you're not concentrating on your work, which is most unusual.'

*Huh!* Daisy thought, stabbing the end of her pen on to the paper and playing with the splodges of ink. Who could possibly get excited about the piece of creative writing Ambler had asked them to do? "An Autumn Scene" was the title. All about leaves turning golden brown and swallows flying south.

Who cared?

Ambler spied the blobs on Daisy's page and for a moment forgot about Maya. She came and picked up the book, keeping it at arm's length.

> "The leeves on the tree
> all went ~~DEE~~ dirty brown.
> It ~~rex~~ rained and
> they fell off.

she read out loud. 'Yes, Daisy; very creative,' she sighed. 'Now if I were to read out Maya's piece, no doubt you'd find out what I *really* wanted.'

For once, when she went back to Maya's desk, she found she was wrong. 'What's this? A blank page?' she quizzed.

'Sorry, Miss. I couldn't think of anything to write.' Maya sounded truly miserable.

Rambler Ambler drew up a chair from an empty desk. 'Now I know that something really *is* the matter,' she said softly, intending the rest of the class to get on with their work.

So Daisy earwigged big time.

'What's wrong?' Ambler insisted. 'Come on, Maya, you can tell me.'

*Like, yeah!* Daisy thought.

'Is there trouble at home? Something you'd like to get off your chest?'

Maya hung her head and said nothing.

'Or is it a problem in school?' The teacher took another wild guess. 'Are you being bullied? Is there something I ought to know?'

*Yuck!* Daisy realised Ambler meant well, but to be honest, she just didn't have the knack. And Maya's eyes were filling with tears again.

Even the teacher saw that it was time to back off. She stood up with a sigh, spied Daisy still flicking ink across her page and launched into a fresh attack. '"Leaves",' she began. 'Spelt L-E-E-V-E-S! And "dirty", spelt D-U-R-T-Y. Now who here can tell Daisy Morelli the correct way to spell these words?'

# Five

'Why isn't "words" spelt W-I-R-D-S?' Daisy asked Maya after school that day. The two girls stood together on the centre line, watching the school team train for Saturday's competition. 'I mean, if "bird" is spelt B-I-R-D, and "word" sounds the same, why isn't it spelt the same?'

'And "burn" has a U, not an I or an O.' Maya admitted that the whole thing was far too confusing.

'Spelling is *pants!*' Daisy declared, making Maya giggle for the first time that day.

'Daisy…' she began, once she could get her face straight again.

'Hmm?' Daisy watched Jimmy, Jared and Kamran sprint up and down the pitch, carefully avoiding the patched sections which Bernie King had roped off with orange and white tape.

'Oh, never mind. It doesn't matter.'

'*What* doesn't matter?'

'Nothing. Forget it.'

Daisy frowned. 'Right, I'll forget it. I don't know what I'm forgetting, but I'm doing it anyway!'

Maya grinned self consciously. 'OK, if I tell you, do you promise to keep it to yourself?'

'Swear!' Daisy agreed eagerly.

'Because I haven't told anyone else. And if this gets out, I'm gonna be dead!'

Daisy's eyes widened. 'Go on!' she squeaked. 'Don't keep me in suspense.'

'It's about the holes…' Maya began. She looked round nervously to check that there was no one nearby. 'You know that Bernie King is accusing Winona's dog?'

Daisy nodded. By this time, her eyes were practically out on stalks. She smelled scandal, drama, a big, big fuss.

'Well, it isn't down to Lulu,' Maya whispered.

'How d'you know?'

'Because!'

'Because what?'

'Because I can see what's going on from the back of my house, can't I?'

Daisy gasped. Of course! Maya's bedroom was like Winona's; it overlooked the school playing field. 'So?' she hissed.

'It was late last night. I was sitting in the dark looking out of the window and I saw who made the two new holes!'

'Wow!' Daisy breathed. The real phantom digger was about to be exposed. 'Who?'

A look of panic flitted across Maya's dark

brown eyes as she gave Daisy the name. 'It was Lennox!' she whispered. 'Bernie's own dog is the one who's to blame!'

'I'd be dead!' Maya insisted. 'Honestly, Daisy – Bernie would kill me if I spread the bad news about his dog!'

The two girls had stayed behind on the playing field long after everyone had left. It was already beginning to turn dark, and a light rain was blowing across the wide empty space.

Daisy stared thoughtfully at the rough, patched pitch. 'What's the worst he could really do?' she wondered.

'Daisy, don't even think about it!' Maya went pale and reminded her of the promise she'd made. 'You said you wouldn't say anything…'

'Yeah, but that was before!'

'Before what?'

'Before I knew!' Daisy grinned as she pictured Fat Lennox digging away in the dark. 'You've got to admit this is one big smack in the chops for Bernie King!'

Big-mouth Bernie – Beefie Bernie the Boss of Woodbridge Junior, whose heavy footsteps made even Mrs Waymann quiver inside her tweedy purple suit. 'Yes, Bernie – no, Bernie!' The headteacher had to follow the caretaker's orders just like everyone else.

If Bernie said it was impossible to open up the school for a jumble sale planned for a Saturday morning, then Waymann had to back down. And she had to keep in his good books over the tiniest details, from replacing light bulbs to stocking up on loo rolls. 'Yes Bernie, no Bernie, three bags full!'

'What are you grinning at?' Winona stopped a few yards away from Maya and Daisy. She'd already been home, changed out of her uniform into a luminous yellow kagoul and come back out to walk Lulu in the rain.

'Daisy, don't say anything!' Maya pleaded quietly.

'But if I told Winona what you just told me,

it would let Lulu off the hook,' Daisy pointed out.

Maya shook her head. 'No. Bernie would just deny it. You know what he's like about Lennox; he thinks he couldn't possibly do anything wrong. And he'd be really mad with me for ever after!'

'True.' Daisy saw the problem. 'We need proof before we finger the real culprit…'

'I said, what were you grinning at?' Winona came up to Daisy with a fierce, pointy expression. 'Haven't you seen a yellow kagoul before?'

'I wasn't laughing at that, honest!' Daisy protested, though she had to admit to herself that Winona's waterproof was very – well, yellow.

'It's better than getting wet!' Winona insisted, head in the air, hood hanging down over her forehead.

'I never said…' Struggling to keep a straight face, Daisy noticed Lulu wander over to the nearest goalpost and sniff hard.

'Hadn't you better keep her on a lead in case Bernie sees her?' she suggested.

'Mind your own business!' Winona snapped, angry to be reminded that her precious pet was currently under a dark cloud of suspicion. She rounded on Daisy before she minced off to fetch Lulu. 'Because if you don't, Daisy Morelli, I might just possibly drop a hint to Miss Ambler that she confiscated your precious Herbie on Friday, and that if she happened to look in her drawer for him, she might get a nasty surprise…!'

'We need proof!' Daisy insisted to Jimmy.

They were walking to school together the next morning, so deep in discussion that they forgot to pester the pigeons on Duke Street. The fat grey birds perched on the park railings and blinked lazily at them as they trotted by.

'But even if we get the proof that Fat Lennox is guilty, what good will it do?' Jimmy shared Maya's opinion that Bernie King would swear black was white when it came to his paunchy pooch.

Daisy looked at him in disgust as she hovered at the kerb waiting for the green man to flash. 'Not you as well!' she sighed. 'How come I'm surrounded by wimps all of a sudden?'

It had taken her ages the previous evening to persuade Maya to let Jimmy in on the Lennox secret. 'Just Jimmy!' she'd wheedled. 'Jimmy won't say a word to anyone, I promise. Anyway, Jimmy's captain of the school soccer team, so he deserves to know the truth about who's digging holes in the pitch!'

In the end Maya had agreed. 'But whatever you and Jimmy decide to do, you've got to keep me out of it,' she'd insisted. 'My mum and dad would be really upset if I got into trouble over this.'

And that had been the deal; Jimmy had the right to know about Lennox, but Maya's name mustn't be dragged into it. 'I promise, cross my heart and hope to die!' Daisy had sworn.

'Who's a wimp?' Jimmy demanded, frowning up at the red man. Traffic crawled by in a steady stream.

'You are. You're scared of Bernie King and his fat dog!' Daisy taunted.

'– Not.'

'– Are.'

'– Not.' Jimmy pressed the button until the man turned to green again. Then he sprinted across the road. 'It's just that we're never gonna get Bernie to admit that Lennox is digging these holes unless we catch it on video or something!'

'Hey!' Daisy caught up with him, her brown eyes alight behind her shaggy fringe. 'Is that brilliant, or what!'

'What?' Jimmy swerved around an old man pushing a bike along the path. He turned the corner on to Woodbridge Road.

Daisy's trainers pounded the pavement

after him. Not a video camera, maybe. But a photograph, definitely. A picture of Fat Lennox digging up the turf. She grinned as they turned through the school gates together. 'I said, you're a genius, Jimmy Black!'

That morning there was a fresh hole to greet them and a scrappy pile of dirt scarring the perfect surface of the caretaker's pitch.

Bernie growled and grumbled. He took out his bucket and spade, patted the earth back into the hole and pressed a square of turf over the top. Then he roped off the area with orange tape.

He even made Mrs Waymann make a stern anouncement in assembly. 'If anyone knows anything about the damage to the playing field, will they please report to Mr King's office at once.'

Squashed between Daisy and Jimmy, Maya blushed hard and stared at the floor.

Waymann's eagle eyes swept around the

hall. 'We must get to the bottom of this mystery as soon as possible,' she said. 'If not, Mr King will make us call off Saturday's competition.'

Sitting in the row behind Jimmy, Kamran let out a gasp of dismay. Jared too was upset. 'That's not fair!' he hissed.

'Be quiet, Daisy!' Ambler snapped from the side of the hall.

Daisy frowned. *Just you wait!* she thought. *When Jimmy and me get the evidence we need, you won't be telling me to shut up – no way!'*

'OK, so how do we take a camera on to the playing field in the middle of the night?' Jimmy quizzed.

It was Wednesday afternoon and the situation was getting desperate.

That morning Bernie had woken up to two more new holes – extra deep and extra wide, with dirty great bones buried in them. He'd gone out to repair them with a face like thunder, Lennox waddling close behind.

'Mr King, I hope you're not going to
continue to accuse poor Lulu!' Mrs Jones had
arrived at school with a miserable looking
Winona. She'd had it out with the caretaker in
front of Daisy, Jimmy and the rest.

'*Poor Lulu!*' Bernie had scoffed, clanking
down his spade and bucket outside his office
door. 'I saw her with my own eyes last
Saturday night, didn't I?'

Mrs Jones had looked down her petite
nose at him. 'If you still think that my little

dog is causing all this damage, then I suggest you go for an eye test!'

And she'd turned on her neat cuban heel and minced off to talk it through with Mrs Waymann.

The headteacher had caved in under the pressure of a visit from Scary Jones. She'd made a clear announcement in assembly that the Jones's poodle was Not Guilty.

'Lulu was locked in the house all night long,' she'd explained. 'So the blame must lie elsewhere!'

Now Bernie King could growl and grumble all he liked, but Winona's pet was off the hook. 'It makes no difference,' he insisted. 'I'll still have to cancel Saturday's competition if this goes on.'

'We need a plan,' Daisy told Jimmy, racing him up Duke Street to the door of his shop. Even she had to admit that snapping Lennox in mid-dig was a tricky challenge.

'Did you hear Bernie sounding off about Saturday?' Jimmy won the race, then paused for breath under a poster advertizing cut-price car seat covers. 'He really meant that stuff about cancelling the competition!'

'That's why we have to act fast.' Daisy thought it through. 'The camera's no problem; I can easily borrow one from my dad. It has a flash that lets you take pictures in the dark. But how do we get into the right position to take the photo? …Hmmm.'

'We could camp!' Jimmy suggested off the top of his head.

Daisy pulled a sour face. 'Yeah; put up a tent on Bernie's precious playing field – NOT!' Then suddenly her face broke into a smile. 'Camp – yeah, brilliant!'

'Yeah?' No one was more surprised than Jimmy at the sudden switch of mood.

'Yeah! Maya and Kamran don't know it yet, but they're gonna invite us to a sleepover at their house this coming Friday. We're gonna ask Mr and Mrs Khan if we can all camp out in their back garden as a special treat… get it?'

Slowly Jimmy nodded. 'Sleepover –

Kamran's place – take your dad's camera with us – yeah.'

Daisy grinned. 'See, you're definitely a super-brain, Jimmy Black!'

And she nipped through the door of Pizza Palazzo to put her soccer-loving pal's plan into action.

# Six

'Dad said yes.' Maya leaned across the aisle
to whisper to Daisy during assembly on
Thursday morning. 'He says we can have the
sleepover tomorrow night!'

'Cool!' Daisy had made the first moves by
phone the night before. At first Maya had
sounded doubtful – her strict dad didn't
usually let her have friends to stay. But
Kamran was his favourite, and when Kamran

added his pleas to Maya's, Mr Khan had given in. Daisy and Jimmy could both come to stay.

' *"Kookaburra sits in the old gum tree-ee,*
*Merry merry king of the woods is he-ee!*
*Laugh-kookaburra, laugh-kookaburra...'*

At the front of the hall Miss Ambler sat with a guitar singing her assembly song in a high, tuneless voice.

' *...Gay your life must be!"* '

'You're sure we can camp out in the garden?' Daisy checked with Maya. She wanted to be certain that their after-dark plan to expose Bernie's dastardly dog could go ahead smoothly.

Maya nodded.

'Ssshhh!' Mrs Hunt hissed, glowering for the first time ever at the quietest pupil in the school.

'There's only one problem,' Maya warned Daisy later.

It was playtime and Daisy, Jimmy and

Maya were marching up and down the sideline, frowning at yet another new hole that had appeared overnight. The pitch was now criss-crossed with Bernie's orange tape to keep kids off the patched areas. At this very moment he was in with Waymann, arguing over whether or not Saturday's matches could take place.

'What's that?' Daisy asked.

'Dad said I had to invite Winona,' Maya confessed.

'Aaagh!' Acting as if she'd been stabbed in the chest, Daisy staggered backwards on to the pitch. 'No, no – please, no!'

*…Blood poured from the wound. For once in her life, Fingers Morelli had been caught napping.*

*Never in a million years had she expected to be double-crossed by a member of her own gang. Sure, she had a hundred hit men from rival mobsters' outfits ready to gun her down the first chance they got. And Fingers was more than ready for them.*

*But not for this sudden stab in the back from the very guy she thought she could trust.*

*As the light of life grew dimmer, she fell to her knees. This was it; the end...*

'Hey, you lot, get off my playing field!' Bernie King yelled as he emerged from the Head's office and stomped across the yard. Fat Lennox trundled along behind.

Daisy ignored him. She collapsed on to Maya. 'Why?' she pleaded, as if with her dying breath.

'Because Winona invited me to her sleepover last week,' Maya explained. 'Dad says it's only fair to invite her back.'

'But she'll ruin everything. She always does!' Daisy yelped. 'What are we gonna do?'

Jimmy wrinkled his snub nose and thought hard. 'Maybe we could drug her drink to keep her quiet,' he suggested.

Daisy gave him a hard stare. 'Shut up, Jimmy!' she snapped.

Just then, Winona herself trotted across with a message from the caretaker. 'Mr King says you lot have to get off his playing field,' she reported smugly. Then she tossed back her golden curls and added, 'Not that it makes much difference any more.'

'What d'you mean?' Jimmy asked, one eye on Lennox.

The dog had swerved away from Bernie, who had passed on the blunt order via Winona then disappeared into his basement office.

Now Lennox was plodding towards the pitch – *huff-huff-puff-puff* – with a sly look on his fat face. *Wheeze-wheeze, hgugh-hgugh* – he sniffed and scrached at the grass by the goalpost.

Daisy held her breath. Maybe – maybe they could catch him in the act of digging right here in broad daylight…

But Lennox was only teasing. He sniffed a bit, scratched a bit, lifted his leg against the goalpost, then changed his mind. With a wink and a wheeze, he trotted off back towards the school.

'Yeah, what d'you mean, it doesn't make much difference?' Daisy pressed Winona for an answer.

'I heard Bernie tell Waymann that Saturday is off!' She dropped the bombshell news with a know-it-all smile. 'Forget the knock-out competition, Jimmy. I got it from the horse's mouth – the whole thing has just been cancelled!'

Was it on or was it off?

'Off!' Winona insisted all through Thursday. She swore that this was what King Bernie had declared.

'On!' said Kamran, who had been in the

secretary's office when Mrs Waymann was talking on the phone to another Headteacher. The message he'd picked up was that the teams should turn up at the school on Saturday as planned.

'Off!' Bernie insisted when Jimmy plucked up the courage to ask him straight out. 'I'm the expert groundsman round here, and what I say goes!'

It came down to who was the boss of Woodbridge Junior.

All day Friday, Bernie stomped around in his caretaker's coat and clompy boots, complaining about untrained dogs and their owners. 'Some people aren't fit to have pets,' he grumbled. 'The dogs round here are out of control – not like my Lennox. Lennox is trained to obey every command. He's the type of dog who won't let you down.'

Lennox wheezed along after him like an old steam train – *huff-huff-huff*.

Meanwhile, Mrs Waymann was under pressure from the other schools. 'Our name will be mud if we cancel the competition,' she reasoned with the caretaker. She smiled and spoke sweetly, promised him double pay to be on duty and let the matches go ahead. Then triple his normal wage – anything to get him to change his mind.

'Hmph!' Surveying his patchwork pitch on Friday evening after school, Bernie King's ears pricked up. 'Three times my basic rate of pay?' he checked. 'Well listen, this is what I'm prepared to do…'

'What did he say?' Jimmy asked Daisy after they'd all arrived at Maya's house for the sleepover. He'd turned up in his football kit, ready for the big day tomorrow, hoping against hope that everything would work out in the end.

Daisy had earwigged on the Head's final

conversation with Bernie then scuttled off with the latest news. 'He says the match is ON...'

'Hurray!' Jimmy jumped and punched the air.

'...If, and only *IF* there are no fresh holes tomorrow morning!' Daisy warned.

She gathered Jimmy, Kamran, Maya, Winona and Lulu around her in the Khans' back garden. They were surrounded by a jumble of groundsheets, poles, tent pegs and sleeping-bags. 'So it's down to us,' she muttered. 'We have to stay awake all night and nail Lennox before he even has chance to dig!'

* * *

10·00 to 11·00pm - Kamran
11·00 to Midnight - Maya
Midnight to 1·00am - Jimmy
1·00 to 2·00am - Daisy

Daisy made a list of who was to stand guard at the bottom of the garden with a torch and camera.

'What about me?' Winona whinged. 'Why don't I get a turn?'

'Oh, sorry!' Daisy chirped, as if she'd forgotten all about Mizz Perfect. Then, 'Are you sure you'll be warm enough standing guard in that thin nightie thing?'

Winona froze her with a haughty look. 'Let me go first,' she insisted.

So Daisy squeezed her name in at the top of the list. 9.00 to 10.00pm – Winona.

'Make sure Lulu stays inside the tent,' she reminded her. 'We don't want her getting in the way and spoiling things.'

A sniff from Winona and a growl from the poodle was all the answer she got.

'So can the others get some sleep while one is on duty?' Jimmy wanted to know. He'd paused from hammering tent pegs into the soft ground to find out how Daisy's plan would work.

'Sure. As long as the look-out manages to stay awake,' Daisy said meaningfully as Winona stretched her mouth open in a wide yawn. 'But if the look-out drops off even for a single minute and lets Lennox dig without taking his picture, we've had it!'

'Yeah, yeah!' Winona looked at her watch, then picked up the torch and camera from the garden seat. 'Lulu, go to sleep!' she ordered the spoiled pooch, who was already snugly curled up on her mistress's sleeping-bag inside the girls' tent.

'Wake Kamran at ten o'clock, remember!' Daisy warned.

'Yeah, yeah!' Tripping lightly to the bottom of the garden, Winona swung the torch beam out across the playing field beyond.

'And if anything happens, make sure you take a photo!' For some reason Daisy felt uneasy about trusting Winona. 'And don't shine that torch everywhere. Mr and Mrs Khan will spot it if you're not careful.'

'Yeah-yeah, yeah-yeah, yeah.' Winona's

long powder blue nightdress stood out in the dark. 'Go to sleep,' she told Daisy. 'Just leave this to me!'

So Daisy crawled into the tent with Maya and Lulu. She took Herbie out of her overnight bag then snuggled him deep inside her sleeping-bag.

'Yeah, I know,' she sighed, as the squidgy hamster gave her one of his wise, silent looks. 'But I didn't invite Winona, did I? So what can I do?'

*Stay awake just in case,* Herbie seemed to suggest. *'Be ready for anything to happen...*

*Zzzzzzz* – Daisy, Maya and Lulu were fast asleep.

In the next tent Jimmy and Kamran were snoring loudly.

*Plip – plip.* Silence. *Plip – plop.*

Daisy jerked awake to the sound of large wet drops splashing on to the roof of the tent. She sat bolt upright.

*Plip-plip-plip-plop-plop! Zzzipp!*
Winona opened the front flap and poked her
head in. 'It's raining!' she wailed.

*Plop-plop-plu-plu-plash.* The drops came
thick and fast.

'I can hear that!' Daisy hissed as Maya
and Lulu slept on. 'Get back on guard in case
Lennox shows up!'

'I'm wet!' Winona moaned, crawling inside
and dripping over Daisy. By this time, the rain
was lashing down on the tent. Maya had

woken up and there were sounds from the boys' tent too.

'What's wrong with a tidgy bit of rain?' Daisy demanded crossly, wriggling out of her bag and grabbing both torch and camera from Winona. Then she scrambled outside.

*Flash – boom!* Lightning ripped through the black sky and thunder crashed. The rain came down in torrents.

'Yerkk, this tent leaks!' Jimmy cried. 'It's pouring in through this big rip!'

'Quick, bail out!' As Kamran leaped into action, the whole tent shook.

'Lulu and I are scared of thunder!' Winona whined. 'We want to go home!'

*Typical!* Stumbling off through the rain towards the fence, Daisy squelched barefoot into mud. She felt her hair stick flat to her head and the cold rain dribble down her neck.

But then, during the next flash of lightning she spotted a four-legged shape – *Boom!* – out in the middle of the playing field – *Flash! Crash!* – digging a giant hole!

Battered by the storm, Daisy pressed on. In the distance, the muddy dog ignored both thunder and lightning.

Behind her, lights went on in Maya's house. The boys' waterlogged tent caved in on top of them and Winona went on wailing.

*Major, major disaster! Girl Struck by Lightning while Photographing Digging Dog!* Daisy could see it all now. *Tragic Boys Drown in Tent! Rescuers Save Two Girls and Poodle from Certain Death!*

Still she ploughed on through the rain. She reached the fence and got the camera ready, pointing the lens at the blurred shape on the pitch. Her hand wobbled at a crash of thunder so loud that it seemed to happen inside her head.

Then *Flash!* Lightning lit up the whole sky with an eerie greenish glow.

The dog left off digging and glanced towards the fence. His bandy legs were caked with mud, his fat white face smeared with dirt.

*Click!* Daisy pressed the button. The

shutter opened and closed. The world returned to darkness.

'Gotcha!' she cried, as Fat Lennox finally took fright and legged it towards the school.

# Seven

'Jimmy-Jimmy-Jimmy! Jim-Jim-Jim!' Winona
led the cheers for Woodbridge Junior's ace
goal-scorer.

'Two-nil, two-nil!' Daisy roared. Their team
had reached the final of the knock-out
competition and were well on their way to
victory.

Maya stood quietly between Winona and
Daisy, wearing a blue and white Woodbridge

scarf and a huge grin.

Jimmy picked the ball out of the back of the net and capered up the pitch.

Or what was left of it. The overnight rain had turned Bernie's perfect playing area into a muddy swamp. Kids slid and skidded, the ball splatted into puddles and the caretaker's neat white lines had all but disappeared.

'How come the King let the matches go ahead?' Leonie had been the first one to come up to Daisy and pose the question. It had been just after lunch and the teams' mini-buses were pulling up on Woodbridge Road.

Daisy, Winona and Maya had been busy mixing orange squash and putting biscuits on to plates for half-time refreshments.

Daisy had given Leonie a wide eyed stare. 'Well...' she'd begun.

First thing that morning Daisy and her team dashed to the chemists and had the reel of film printed. She opened the envelope of photographs with shaky fingers.

'Please let it turn out OK!' Jimmy breathed.

Daisy flicked through pictures of Mia sitting, Mia crawling, Mia smiling, Mia crying…

'Come on!' Kamran urged. 'Get to the one of Lennox!'

…Mia covered in chocolate, Mia ready for bed in stripey pyjamas…

'It's no good. The one of Lennox didn't come out!' Winona whimpered.

*No thanks to you,* Daisy thought. She came to the very last photo in the pile.

Fat Lennox's ugly mug stared out at them. Rain dripped from his floppy ears. His piggy eyes were mean and his slobbery mouth hung open in guilty surprise.

'Yes!' Jimmy clenched his fist in a victory salute.

Daisy felt her heart race. Here was the evidence they needed. A dog – *the* dog – Bernie King's *own* dog – digging a hole in the pitch to bury a bone!

She turned to Maya in triumph. 'Thanks for this!'

Maya shook her head. 'I didn't do anything.'

But Daisy argued back. 'Yes you did. You stuck your neck out and told me about Lennox. A lot of people would just have kept quiet. Then you fixed up the sleepover.'

'Yeah,' Jimmy agreed. 'Thanks, Maya!'

'Yeah, thanks!' Kamran and even Winona echoed.

A warm glow crept over their shy friend's face. But she said nothing at all.

'No can do!' Bernie King stormed down the corridor ahead of Mrs Waymann.

Daisy had volunteered to have the showdown while the others waited outside school. It was eleven o'clock on Saturday morning; two and a half hours before the football competition was due to start. She stood in the main entrance and watched the clash between Beefy Bernie and the Head. For the time being, there was no sign of Lennox.

'But can't you fill in this last hole and let the matches go ahead as planned?' Waymann pleaded.

'Like I said, no can do,' he insisted. 'I've gone as far as I can go!'

Waymann sighed and tried again. 'The children will be so disappointed.'

'Well, they'll have to get used to it. I told you yesterday; one more hole in my pitch and our deal was off!'

Daisy smiled to herself and took the photo

out of her pocket.

She waited until Mrs Waymann gave up and retreated into her office. And until Bernie had whistled for his dog and Lennox had come lumbering up the steps from the yard.

Lennox saw Daisy and faltered. His shifty little eyes were filled with guilt.

'Yeah, that's right. The game's up!' Daisy hissed, bracing herself to stand up to Bernie.

*Huff-huff-hoogh!* Lennox wheezed heavily and plonked himself down on the door mat.

Daisy advanced towards the dog's master. She shoved the photograph in front of his face.

'And what did Bernie say?' Leonie had asked after Daisy had brought her up to date.

Daisy had crunched her way through a custard cream. 'Nothing,' she'd replied. 'Big fat zero. He just went white and stared at the photo in total shock!'

'And what about Lennox?' Leonie had enjoyed the vision of the bulldog caught red-handed.

'He wheezed like crazy, playing for sympathy, I guess. But Bernie came down on him pretty hard. He told him he was a no-good, useless, idle so-and-so…'

'Stop, or I'll feel sorry for the stupid mutt!' Leonie had giggled.

'…A disgrace, a major let-down, a great big brainless idiot!'

'Poor Lennox!' Leonie had doubled up laughing.

'Poor Lennox, nothing!' Winona had cut in. 'That dog deserves everything that's coming!'

Daisy had gone on to explain to Leonie that, after Bernie had ranted and raved, he'd marched straight off to the High Street. 'He made a beeline for the butchers shop, asked them if they'd been giving bones to his dog. When they said yes, he went barmy with them too.'

Leonie had nodded. 'But anyway he had to back down over the football competition?'

'Yep. I made him promise to keep Lennox

in at night from now on. If he did, then we wouldn't go public and point the finger at his dog. Lennox's nasty habit would be kept quiet.'

'Clever!' Leonie had approved. 'And that's how you also got him to agree to let the competition go ahead?'

Cheeks full of custard creams, Daisy had grinned. 'Neat, huh? Bernie couldn't face the disgrace. He backed down just in time to stop Waymann from ringing the other schools to cancel.'

'And here we are!' Winona had chirped, arranging caramel wafers in a fan shape on the plate.

'Jimmy-Jimmy-Jimmy! Two-nil, two-nil!'

Five minutes to go in the final play-off against All Saints First School.

Parents packed the sidelines, cheering their kids on. Winona jumped up and down, and chanted her team towards cup triumph.

Jimmy, Jared, Kamran and the rest played

their hearts out.

And Daisy's dad was there to put the whole thing on record.

*Click-click!* Gianni took a photo of a mud-caked Jimmy attacking the goalmouth. *Click!* A picture of the All Saints goalie at full stretch to save the shot.

'Good save!' he shouted, then went on clicking.

'Huh, it should've been three!' Daisy muttered to Herbie. She'd brought her hamster along to enjoy the match.

*Two's enough.* Herbie's one-eyed stare warned her not to be greedy.

'Isn't this wonderful?' Miss Ambler came along in her scarf, woolly hat and wellies.

'*Maginifico!*' Gianni agreed, aiming then capturing the excited teacher on camera.

Rambler-Ambler turned to Daisy. 'Mrs Waymann tells me that you managed to get Mr King to change his mind,' she began. Then she spotted Herbie's head poking out of Daisy's top pocket. She blinked hard then looked again. 'Erm – Daisy, dear – surely I – I mean, didn't I…?'

Daisy gulped and squashed Herbie out of sight.

'Yes, that's right; you did confiscate Herbie during the art lesson,' Winona broke in brightly.

*Eyes of newt, toes of frog* – Daisy gritted her teeth and thought witchy thoughts.

'But you gave him back to Daisy earlier this week!' Winona assured the puzzled teacher.

'I did?' Ambler looked confused.

*She did?* Daisy was slow to catch on.

'Yes. Don't you remember? It was when I helped you clear out your drawer, and you told me that Herbie was cluttering the place up, so Daisy might as well have him back.'

'Ah!' The teacher smiled vaguely, then wandered on. 'Yes, I expect you're right, Winona, dear.'

'Close!' Daisy muttered. Whatever else you said about Winona-Goody-Goody-Jones, you had to admit she was a brilliant liar.

*Whheeeeepp!* The referee blew the final

whistle. Woodbridge had won the cup!

Jimmy gave Kamran a muddy hug. Then
the team hoisted him on to their shoulders.

Gianni clicked while the fans cheered.
'*Magnifico!*' he cried. 'Well done, Jimmy!'

As the shouts and cheers died down,
Daisy's dad tucked his camera into its case.
He tousled Daisy's mop of dark hair and told
her it was time to go home.

'Yuck, don't do that!' Daisy hissed,
shooting out of reach.

'I suppose you'll be cooking for the whole
family tonight?' Winona chipped in before
they left. 'You and Mrs Morelli, baby Mia,
Daisy…'

Gianni nodded and smiled. '*Pizza
Napoletana*, just like my *momma* makes!'

'Ah yes!' Winona breezed on. 'Your
mother…'

Daisy cringed. Shut up, Winona! Don't
you dare!

Winona looked bright as a canary in her
shiny yellow kagoul. 'Is Mrs Morelli senior
enjoying her visit to England?'

*Drop dead, Win-oh-na!* Daisy snarled
under her breath, then shot off ahead.

Gianni frowned. 'A visit from my momma?'
He stared suspiciously after his galloping
daughter. 'Daisy, come back!'

But she'd vanished amongst the legs and
arms of the winning team. She was slapping

Jimmy on the back, secretly swearing to kill Winona. 'Two-nil!' she crowed.

She was knee-deep in mud, in trouble again – and happy!

Look out for other Definitely Daisy
adventures!

# Just you wait, Winona!

## Jenny Oldfield

Winona's a goody goody who sticks like
glue and threatens to ruin Daisy's street
cred. Daisy can't deal with a teacher's
pet hanging around - until classmate
Leonie invites her to convert Winona into
one of the gang. It's a hard challenge -
but Daisy's determined to try...